Race to the Rescue

Adapted by Steve Foxe
Based on the episode "The Need for Speed"
written by Mairghread Scott

LITTLE, BROWN & COMPANY
LB kids

D1406969

Little, Brown and Company

Hachette Book Group
1290 Avenue of the Americas, New York, NY 10104
Visit us at lb-kids.com

LB kids is an imprint of Little, Brown and Company.
The LB kids name and logo are trademarks of Hachette Book Group, Inc.

The publisher is not responsible for websites (or their content) that are not owned by the publisher.

First Edition: November 2016

ISBN 978-0-316-39378-2

Library of Congress Control Number: 2016945697

10 9 8 7 6 5 4 3 2 1

CW

Printed in the United States of America

Licensed By:

The Rescue Bots are a group of Transformers who protect and serve the humans of Griffin Rock.
Heatwave leads the team. Chase, Blades, and Boulder are part of the original crew, while Blurr is one of the new recruits!

Heatwave needs Blurr's help with an emergency. Kade is stuck in the middle of a toxic waste spill! Blurr rushes to the rescue.

"Slow down!" Heatwave shouts.
But it's too late for Blurr to stop.

The Autobot spins out of control and splashes toxic sludge all over Kade! Blurr panics—until he sees Kade smile and eat some of the goo. It's not toxic waste—it's cake frosting!

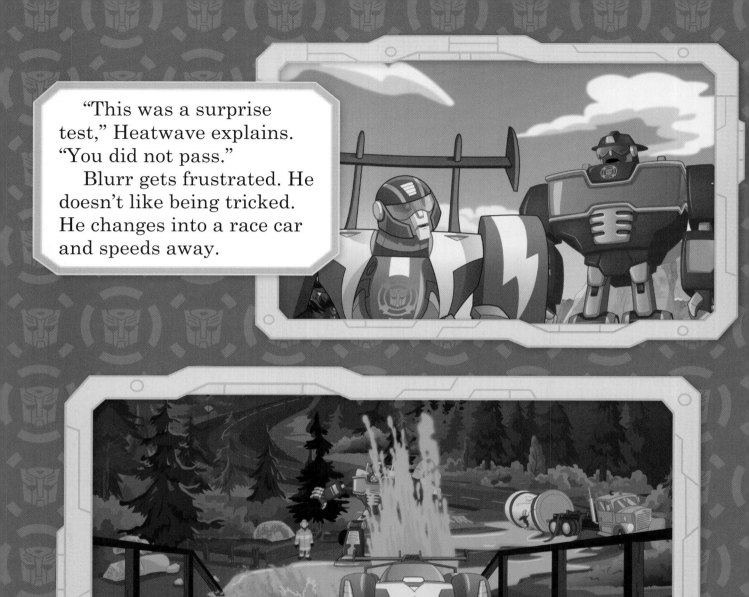

"This was a surprise test," Heatwave explains. "You did not pass."

Blurr gets frustrated. He doesn't like being tricked. He changes into a race car and speeds away.

As he zooms through the streets of Griffin Rock, Blurr finds graffiti written in Cybertronian. The Autobot follows the sound of spray painting nearby and spots a strange figure in the shadows.

"Another test already, Heatwave?" Blurr asks. "I will not fail again!" He calls for backup and races off to catch the criminal.

Blurr chases the round Bot through the streets and right into an Autobot ambush!

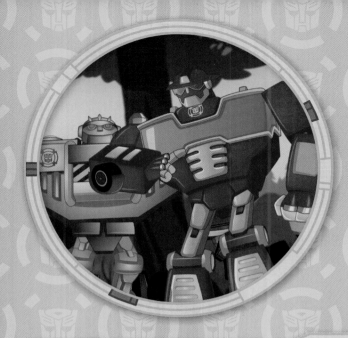

"It's a Mini-Con!" Boulder says. Heatwave tries to blast the menace with his nozzles, but the Mini-Con spits water back into Heatwave's face!

The Mini-Con, named Bounce, smashes through a nearby truck and spills laughing gas into the streets!

"We'll deal with the gas," Heatwave says to Blurr. "You go catch that Con!"

Blurr shifts into high gear. Out of nowhere, a red sports car knocks Blurr off the road!

"No way is a human stealing my rescue," Blurr says.

But the red sports car isn't being driven by a human—it changes into an Autobot!

"Time for you to go back to jail, Bounce!" the red Autobot shouts at the Mini-Con.

When Blurr finally catches up, he is confused to see Bounce with another Autobot. The red stranger mistakes Blurr for a Decepticon and launches a flying kick!

While the two Autobots fight, Bounce escapes!

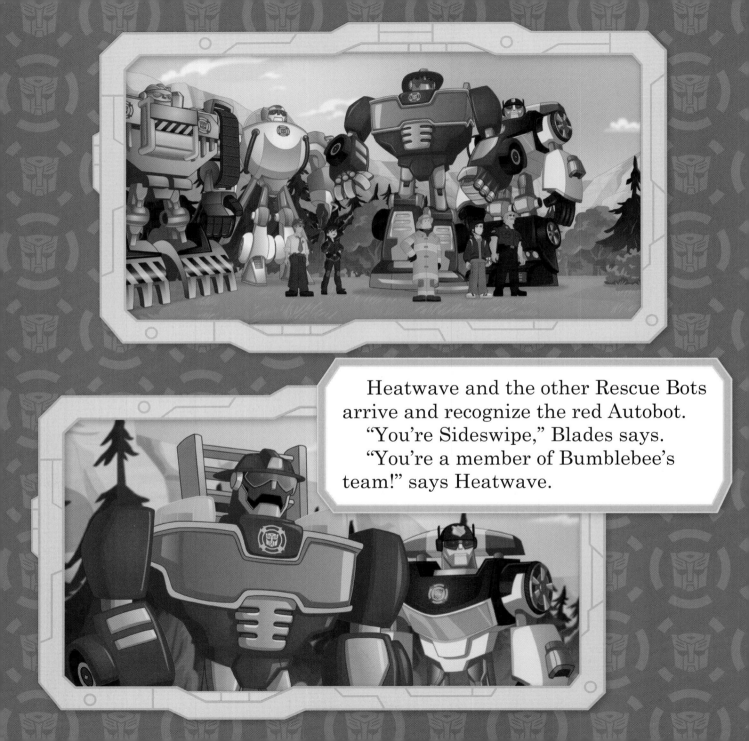

Heatwave and the other Rescue Bots arrive and recognize the red Autobot.

"You're Sideswipe," Blades says.

"You're a member of Bumblebee's team!" says Heatwave.

With the confusion cleared up, the Autobots return to the firehouse. Sideswipe explains that Bounce escaped custody and jumped through a Groundbridge to Earth.

Blurr is jealous that Sideswipe chases after criminals instead of waiting around to rescue humans in danger.

"Maybe you should join Bumblebee's team," Sideswipe says. "If you're fast enough to catch Bounce, that is."

"You can decide your place after the mission," Heatwave says. "Rescue Bots, roll to the rescue!"

The team sets up a trap to catch Bounce. But it's up to Sideswipe and Blurr to trick the Mini-Con into getting caught.

Bounce leads the Bots on a high-speed chase. Blurr skids out of control and nearly crashes into a crowded café!

Luckily, Sideswipe tackles Blurr at the last second, saving the people. But Bounce escapes into the sewers.

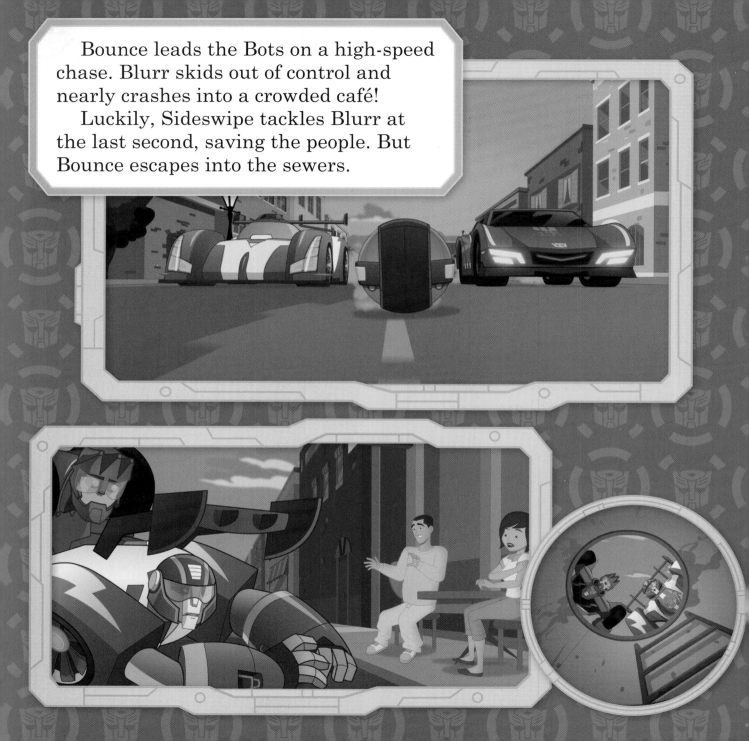

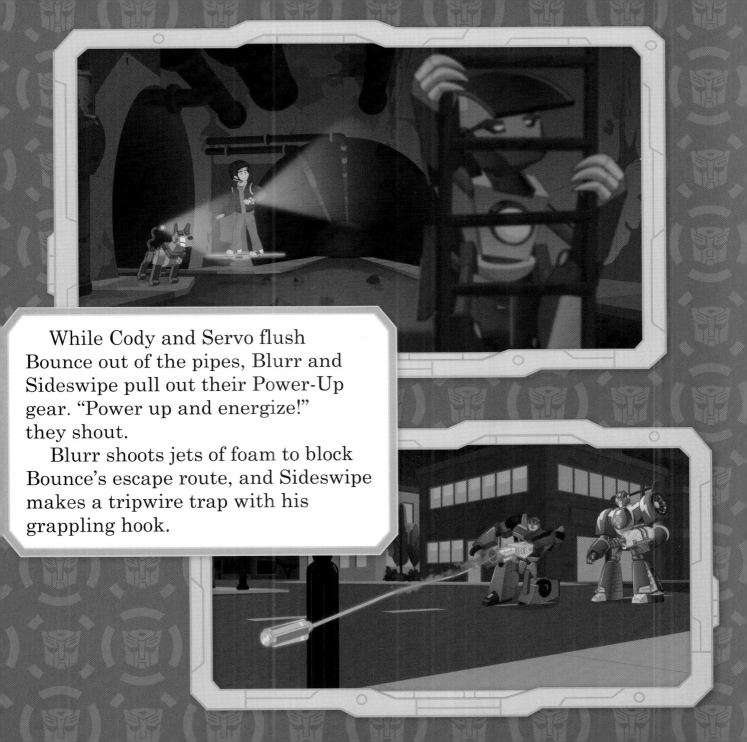

While Cody and Servo flush Bounce out of the pipes, Blurr and Sideswipe pull out their Power-Up gear. "Power up and energize!" they shout.

Blurr shoots jets of foam to block Bounce's escape route, and Sideswipe makes a tripwire trap with his grappling hook.

Bounce is cornered!
"Stand back, Sideswipe," Blurr says. "Bounce is all mine—and so is a spot on Bumblebee's team!"

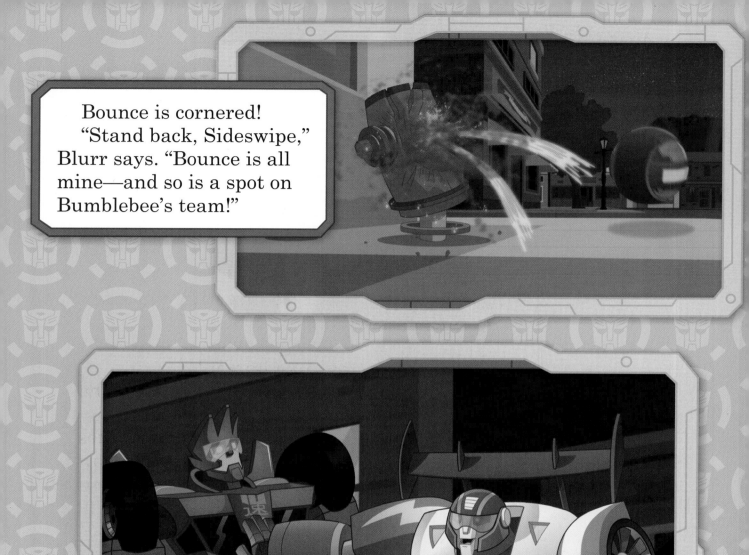

Before Blurr can nab the Mini-Con, Bounce knocks over a lamppost, which starts to fall toward a human!

"Look out!" Blurr yells. The speedy Autobot abandons his pursuit of Bounce and rescues the innocent human from harm.

Just then, a speeding car turns the corner! Blurr acts fast and stops the vehicle with his foam gear as the other Rescue Bots capture Bounce.

Blurr feels like a failure. "I missed my one shot to join Bumblebee's squad," Blurr says.

But Heatwave claps Blurr on the back. "That's because you're a natural-born rescuer!" he says. "You just saved two humans without even thinking!"

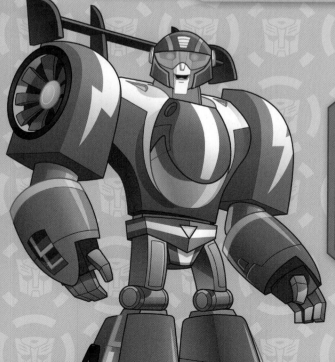

Blurr feels better. After some thought, he makes up his mind. "I am not sure I can go any faster than I do now," Blurr says, "but I know that if I train harder, I can become a better Rescue Bot!"